Christian's Journey

To Karl Alexander: May all of your life be a Christian's journey!

Chariot Victor Publishing
A division of Cook Communications, Colorado Springs, Colorado 80918
Cook Communications, Paris, Ontario
Kingsway Communications, Eastbourne, England

Christian's Journey
©1998 by Chariot Victor Publishing for text and illustrations

Executive Editor, Karl Schaller • Adapted by Karl Schaller
Written and Edited by Karl Schaller, Lee Hough, Liz Duckworth
Designed by Andrea Boven • Illustrations by Drew Rose

CIP Applied For
First Printing, 1998
Printed in Singapore
ISBN: 0-78143-053-4
1 2 3 4 5 6 7 8 9 10 Printing/Year 02 01 00 99 98

Chariot Victor Publishing
A Division of Cook Communications

Part One

On the long drive to church, Christian gloomily stared out the car window. Even the music blasting from his headphones couldn't lift his spirits. *What was the point of going to church*, he wondered, *when God had let him down so badly?*

Christian tried to block out the last time he saw his grandpa's face—two short weeks ago. *I loved you, Grandpa*, he thought. *I prayed that God would save your life. But you died. Why didn't God answer my prayer?*

Confusion was all he felt as the car pulled into the church lot.

"Well, well ... it's the Trueman family," greeted Pastor Heart. "How are you, Chris?"

Unsure of what to say, Chris lowered his eyes and sprinted past the pastor's outstretched hand. He could just hear the worry in his mother's quiet voice. "I'm sorry, Pastor. Christian doesn't want to come to church lately. He's been acting this way since his grandfather died."

Christian settled into the back row of his Sunday School class. He smiled as he remembered his grandpa as a good man who had often talked about his love for Jesus.

His thoughts were interrupted. "Is this seat taken?" It was his friend Hope, pointing to the chair next to him. Her eyes, as usual, were smiling.

"Uh ... help yourself," said Chris. He wondered if Hope might understand his questions about God. *Probably not*, he thought, sinking lower in his chair.

Before Sunday School was over, Chris decided there was no way he would sit through the church service too. But where could he go instead?

The minute class ended, Christian snuck down the basement stairs, hoping no one would see him. Suddenly his foot slipped on a loose board and he fell, hitting his head hard enough to see stars. He sat up to shake off the pain while strange shapes slowly came into focus. Boxes, old pews, and dusty cobwebs filled the shadowy room.

Narrow
is
the
Path

Chris was drawn to an old pulpit standing in the center of the room's clutter. It looked ancient, giving off a mysterious glow in the gloomy darkness. Chris couldn't help climbing up into it. Suddenly he heard a giggle coming from the basement stairs.

A wave of panic gripped Christian as he realized that he had been caught.

Hope emerged from the stairs' shadows. "I hope you're not mad that I followed you. You looked so down in Sunday School, I thought I'd better make sure you were okay."

"Hey, I'm fine!" said Chris. *Did that sound angry?* he wondered. "Wanna help me check this out?" he added more kindly.

Part Two

As they studied the pulpit, Chris realized there were words carved into the front. He read them out loud to Hope: "Narrow is the path." No sooner had the words left his lips, than the floor beneath the pulpit began to shake.

"What—" Chris' words were swallowed up by the noise of the floor cracking. Hope and Chris fell into a long, dark passageway.

"Are you okay?" Christian asked Hope, brushing the dirt from his clothes.

"I'm okay, but where are we?" Hope replied. looking around anxiously. "Did we fall through the basement floor?"

Before he could answer, Chris noticed a man walking toward them.

"Greetings," said the man, who was dressed very oddly. "I have been expecting you. My name is Parson. Welcome to Chapelville. You must be Hope and Chris."

"You ... you ... have been expecting us?" Christian sputtered in surprise.

Hope began to tremble in fear. "Who are you? Where are we? I want to go home!"

"I know, Hope," said Parson gently. "And to get home, you must follow the Narrow Path to the Celestial City. Chris, you must follow that same path. There you will discover what you need to know about your grandpa."

"Please don't be afraid," Parson continued. "I 'm here to help. And my friends will help you too." Out of nowhere, two bright little angels appeared.

"The Shining One's our name, and adventure is our game," they rapped.

"I'm called Cornelius," said the dark-haired cherub.

"And I'm Denzel," said the other. "When you need help, just call."

At that, they both disappeared, leaving Chris to wonder if he had truly seen them at all.

Part Three

"Come on, Chris," begged Hope. "Let's go!" Following Parson, she tugged on Christian's arm, pulling him to the gate that guarded the Narrow Path.

Christian heard running footsteps and whirled around. "My name is Stubborn," said a boy, who was nearly out of breath. "This is my friend Wishy-Washy. Do you know the way to Celestial City? We're lost."

Chris answered, "Sure! That's where we're going. Do you want to come with us on the Narrow Path?" He began to push open the gate.

Stubborn pointed at the Path. "That can't be the right way. It's too narrow ... and rocky. It looks like a hard trip. I'll just find my own way." He ran off.

"What about you, Wishy-Washy?" Hope asked.

"No thanks! Oh ... well ... I guess I'll come along," said the girl with a shrug.

The four travelers walked uphill on the Narrow Path for hours. Finally, Hope gasped, "I'm so tired. Let's turn back."

Wishy-Washy whined, "Yeah, I want to give up." Just then, she and Hope stumbled and started sinking into brown, sticky mud.

"Chris ... Parson ... help!" cried Hope. Christian reached for Hope, but as he did, he too was sucked into the deep mud.

As Christian struggled, he heard Hope pray. "Help us, God. Please save us."

"Praying won't work," he said, remembering his grandpa. "God doesn't hear you."

But Hope's prayer *was* answered. Cornelius and Denzel appeared, pulled the travelers out of the swampy mud, and set them on solid ground.

"God answered your prayer by sending us," said Denzel.

"It must have been awful in Give Up Swamp," added Cornelius.

"Give Up Swamp?" repeated Chris. "This place is getting stranger all the time!"

"Yes, you were stuck," Cornelius explained. "You were tired, cold, and ready to give up, right?" Hope nodded in agreement.

"I can't take anymore of this," cried Wishy-Washy, suddenly bursting into tears. "Let me out of here!" And off she ran, downhill, back toward the Narrow Path gate.

"Parson, what will happen to her?" asked Hope, sounding worried.

Parson patted his Bible. "Well, Jesus told a story about people like Wishy-Washy. He said that a farmer threw some seed on rocky soil. It grew quickly but had no strong roots. As soon as the sun got too hot, the tiny plants died. Wishy-Washy is like that seed. She believed in God, but only when everything was going right. When things got tough, her faith withered and she ran away."

Christian thought about Parson's words and his own lack of faith. He would have a lot more thinking to do on the long road home.

Part Four

The next morning, Chris, Parson, and Hope continued on their way to Celestial City.

Along came a man riding one horse and leading another. Dismounting, he swept off his hat and bowed deeply. "Good morning, pilgrims. Allow me to introduce myself. I am Sir Worldly Wise." The words rolled off his tongue like honey.

Sir Worldly Wise continued, "I want to offer the two young travelers my extra horse. The path ahead is so rough, I know my horse will make the ride easier." A sly smile slid across his face.

"Beware, children," Parson warned. "His words seem right, but his path does not lead to Celestial City."

But Christian was running out of patience. "A quick, easy ride to Celestial City sounds great. Let's go, Hope!"

So the two young people rode away with Sir Wordly Wise, leaving Parson behind.

The travelers' first stop was a town called Vanity Fair. Christian was amazed at all the merchants selling fantastic toys. He and Hope saw jugglers and puppet shows, and listened to wonderful musicians. With money from Sir Worldly Wise, they bought all the candy they wanted. Caught up in so much excitement, they soon forgot all about The Celestial City. And they failed to notice that Sir Worldly Wise had disappeared into the crowded town.

As they were walking through the streets, enjoying the delights of Vanity Fair, Chris and Hope met Selfish, Lazy Bones, and Suspicion.

"Tell me," said Hope to the kids, "who owns this place?"

Selfish smirked. "The Dragon owns Vanity Fair," she said. "He set the town up centuries ago. It's great! At Vanity Fair we live a little and forget a lot." Everyone laughed.

But Suspicion spoke in a hushed voice. "Beware of the Dragon." His words hung in sudden silence.

Christian caught Hope's eye and saw that she was frowning. "Come on, Hope. It's time to go."

Leaving Vanity Fair wasn't as easy as it seemed. Though they searched and searched, they couldn't find the Narrow Path.

Wishing he knew what to do, Chris suddenly felt a hot wind on his back.

"Run, Chris, run!" Hope shouted. "It's the Dragon!"

Part Five

Frozen with fear, Christian remembered how prayer had helped them at Give Up Swamp, but he wasn't sure that God would answer *his* prayer. He could only try. "Oh God," he prayed," protect us from the Dragon!"

Sent by God, the Shining Ones arrived. Looking like firefighters, with helmets and hoses, they drenched the Dragon with a stream of water. The Dragon backed away. The angels then helped the kids to safety.

Christian breathed a huge sigh of relief.

The angels said together "In order to return to the Narrow Path, you will now have to go through the Valley of Darkness."

Hope and Chris groaned.

"You won't really be alone. God will be with you. And we will give you a suit of spiritual armor for protection."

Denzel pulled a scroll from behind his back, cleared his throat, and began to read. "Put on the full armor of God so that you can be safe against the devil."

Will this armor really work? wondered Chris.

Although the little angels had promised safety, Chris still trembled as he and Hope entered the Valley of Darkness. Each step was slow and heavy as they moved further into the deep shadows.

"Chris, what's that light?" asked Hope.

Christian looked up just in time to see a flaming arrow headed toward him. "Your shield, Hope. Use your shield!"

Hope and Chris held their shields over their heads as the arrows rained down on them. Each arrow carried a message carved in its wooden shaft: "Don't read the Bible." "Don't pray." "Don't go to church." "Don't tell your friends about God."

As soon as the arrows stopped, Chris and Hope were surrounded by tiny dragons. They circled the two and began an evil chant. "God doesn't love you. The Bible is make-believe."

The young people covered themselves with their shields and continued to slash with their swords. They prayed, "Jesus, *You* are Lord."

When they finally peeked out from behind their shields, the dragons were gone. Chris felt Hope poking him. "Chris! Look! It's the end of the darkness."

Part Six

Christian opened his eyes to see the welcome sight of the Shining Ones.

"I told you they would make it," said Denzel, giving Cornelius a high-five.

Hope shuddered. "I'm so glad God brought us out of that thick, scary darkness."

The two travelers hardly had the energy to stand, so Denzel and Cornelius half-carried them to an enormous, white house. The mansion was surrounded by colorful flower beds. Hope and Chris rubbed their eyes. They could hardly believe what they saw.

"Welcome! Welcome!" shouted four beautiful girls from the porch.

Christian read the sign by the front door: Welcome to the Refreshing Resort. The girls ushered their visitors in. Each wore a long white dress. Their flowing hair was woven with daisies and peaceful smiles lit their faces.

"I'm Kindness," said the oldest girl. "And these are my sisters: Joy, Purity, and Love. The Resort is God's gift to the weary traveler. Can you stay and rest awhile?"

"Not for long," answered Hope. "We really need to be getting home."

"What's the hurry?" asked Chris. "This looks like the perfect place to get some rest from this road trip."

After lunch, Chris found himself telling story after story to his willing listeners. The sisters seemed to hang on his every word about the amazing journey.

Several times Hope started to interrupt his stories, but Christian was enjoying himself too much to stop. "Thank you, God. This is a great place," Christian said. He didn't notice when Hope stood to leave.

She muttered, "Maybe *you're* in no hurry to get back, but I'm going *now*." She slipped out of the house and headed back to the Narrow Path.

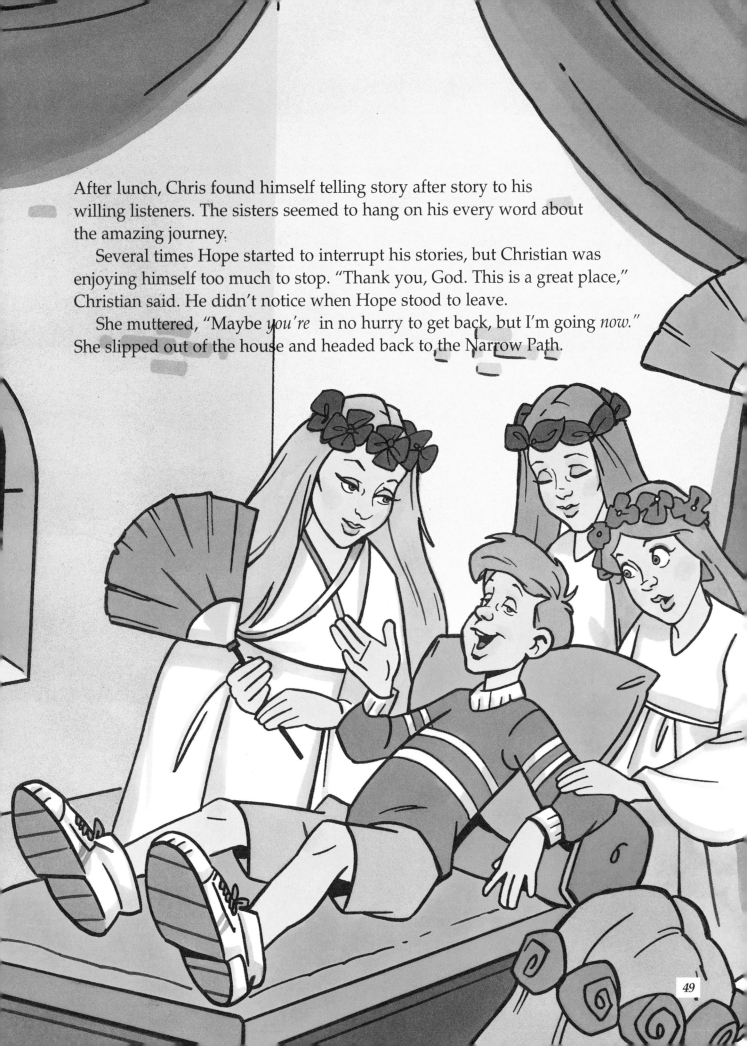

As she walked, Hope felt anger growing inside her. Why didn't Chris care as much about hurrying to finish the journey as she did? *He never thinks about my feelings,* she fumed.

After awhile, Hope wandered to another enormous mansion. The gatekeeper there called to her. "We have lots of rooms for the night."

Hope thought, *I'll show that Chris. I don't need him or anybody else to get home.* She marched up to the gatekeeper and said, "I'll take a room for the night."

Though the mansion looked fine outside, inside it was dark and full of frightening shadows.

Before she knew what was happening, the Gatekeeper had opened a door to a room that looked like a prison. Shoving her down the steps, he said harshly, "Here is your room. Welcome to Doubting Castle."

The old man slammed the door and locked it from the outside. Then he hung the key on the wall—beyond her reach.

"What have I done now?" Hope wailed. "I doubted my friend Chris." She collapsed in tears on the dirty floor.

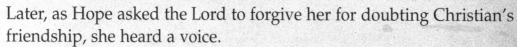

Later, as Hope asked the Lord to forgive her for doubting Christian's friendship, she heard a voice.

"Chris! Is that you?" she asked.

"Yeah!" Chris whispered. "The Shining Ones and I have been searching all over for you. We've been worried!"

Hope saw that Chris was at the door's window, handing through the key he found outside on the wall. She grabbed it and the two quickly escaped the Doubting Castle. "You're a true friend," Hope said to Chris.

They tiptoed past the snoring gatekeeper and didn't stop until they were again on the Narrow Path. They were both happy to discover Parson waiting there.

Part Seven

On and on the travelers climbed, passing Delightful Mountain and Pleasure Palace. Finally, they rounded a corner and saw, gleaming before them, The Celestial City.

"Unbelievable!" gasped Hope.

"Wow!" Christian was amazed at the city's beauty. He found himself praying as he walked, "Lord, I think I know the reasons why you wanted me to take this journey. I've learned so much about trusting You and talking to You."

As they walked on, they came upon a wide, dangerous river. "This is the River of Trial," said Parson. "You must cross it. Only your trust in God will get you across."

Parson crossed the river right away.

Hope took a deep breath. "Jesus, help me to trust in You as I cross this river. I'm scared and I need you." The water deepened, and Hope was forced to swim. She safely reached the sandy shore at the other side.

As he jumped in, Christian wondered if he could make it. The water was cold and rushing with great speed. He began to thrash in the water, gasping for breath. "Help!" he called. "Jesus, please help me!" Still shouting and flailing his arms, Chris finally touched dry land.

Denzel, Cornelius, and Parson all rushed to pull him ashore.

"You did it!" shouted Hope, hugging Chris tightly.

"God did it," Christian said with a soft smile.

Now tired and wet, Chris and the others could see a tall, golden gate ahead. A man stood there. Chris could hardly believe his eyes. "Grandpa?" He ran and hugged his grandfather.

"Well done, Christian," said Grandpa. "You have learned much on your journey. Jesus loves you, and He did hear your prayer about me. It was my time to go and be with God, you see, and He has healed me for forever. I am so happy here."

Chris felt his heart would burst with happiness.

"And now you must return home," Grandpa said. "You still have work to do in Everytown."

Christian gave his grandfather one last hug. He suddenly felt a strong wind swirling around him.

"Trust Jesus always, Christian," Grandpa called.

Parson and the Shining Ones waved goodbye to Chris and Hope. Suddenly the wind knocked both Chris and Hope off their feet. Hope called out, "We're falling—" and then her voice faded from Christian's ears.

The next thing he heard was, "Christian, wake up!"

Chris was lying on the basement floor, looking up into the faces of his mother, father, and Hope. "Are you all right, Chris?" Hope asked. "I got your folks as soon as I found you here."

"I'm okay—just a little groggy," said Christian. *The journey to Celestial City ... was it only a dream? It seemed so real!* Then Chris remembered his grandpa.

"Mom! Dad! Now I know that God really does hear my prayers. And He's taking good care of Grandpa."

His mother smiled. "We know, dear. We know. Now are you ready to come upstairs?"

Chris was filled with joy as he, his family, and Hope went upstairs to the church service. While he and Hope joined in a song of praise, Christian knew that the trust in his heart would stay with him—wherever his life's journey might lead.

Faith Parenting
Guide
Christian's Journey

AGE: 4-7 Read to Me; 8+ Read it Myself
LIFE ISSUE: My child doesn't understand that prayer is simply talking with God.
VALUE: Prayer

PARENT INTERACTIVITY: - Read the book with your child and then interact with your child using the different ways a child learns.

👁 **VISUAL LEARNING STYLE:** - Show your child the pictures in each section of the story and ask him/her the discussion starters listed below. Pray together after each discussion time.

👂 **AUDITORY LEARNING STYLE:** - Go to a deeper discussion with each discussion starter.

PART 1 INTRO TO PRAYER
To begin the story, Christian is upset that God didn't answer his prayer to let his grandpa live. Ask your child if he or she ever prayed to God without a clear answer. Share times in your life when God has answered and when He hasn't.

PART 2 GUARDIAN ANGELS
In Part 2, Christian and Hope meet new friends. Explain to your children that a "Parson" is another name for pastor. Also, explain that God provides guardian angels for protection at important times in our lives. Ask your child if he or she has ever seen an angel. Of course, they will say no. Have fun sharing what you both think angels might look like. Read Psalm 91:11.

PART 3 THE WILL TO DO RIGHT
Tell your child that sometimes in life, the right way can be the hard way, and they shouldn't give up doing what's right. This exemplifies the Building Block of perseverance. It was only when Hope wanted to give up, that she fell into Give Up Swamp. "Blessed is the person who perseveres under trial, because when he has stood the test, he will receive the crown of life that God has promised to those who love him." James 1:12

PART 4 TEMPTATION TO DO WRONG
There are many people who will play the role of Sir Worldly Wise in any person's life: one who tempts another from the right path to the easy, wrong path. Share with your child how logical and convincing these people will be. But God's way is always the right way.

PART 5 THE FULL ARMOR OF GOD
Read to your child Ephesians 6:14-17 about putting on the full Armor of God daily. Discuss with him or her what each part of the armor plays in the life of a Christian.

PART 6 FRIENDSHIP
Hope doubted Christian's friendship and commitment to get to the Celestial City. Because of her doubt, she was jailed in Doubting Castle. Ask your child, if he or she gets mad at friends and for what reasons. Read to your child about the friendship between David and Jonathan in 1 Samuel 20.

PART 7 TALKING TO GOD
Have fun talking to your child about prayer. As Christian learned, prayer is talking to God during the tough times and good times. Christian also learned that God doesn't always answer prayer the way that we want. But we must have faith that God hears our prayer and loves us. "The prayer of a righteous person is powerful and effective." James 5:16

✋ **TACTILE LEARNING STYLE:** - Do a Building Block Object Lesson. Using the furniture in your home, create a mazelike obstacle course. Then blindfold your child to guide him or her through the course by voice commands. When you stop talking the child should stop walking.
Ask your child, "Can you think of how this game might relate to prayer?"
SHARE: In order to get through this maze, you had to listen to the voice of someone who could see the maze. In order to get through the maze of life, or to understand what God wants you to do each day, you need to listen to what God is telling you.
You need to be in constant communication with God through prayer.

Excerpted from Family Night Tool Chest, Christian Character Qualities, Weidman/Bruner, Chariot Victor Publishing, 1997